Other books in this series:

What Could You Do?
For preschoolers

Defeat Bullies and Bad-Guys:
Kids Can Face the 7 People-Dangers
-includes lesson plans for elementary counselors
and other teachers!

Facing the 7 People-Dangers
       for Middle School Girls
       for Middle School Boys
       for Young Men
       for Adult Women
       for Adult Men

Not Prey:

Facing the
7 People-Dangers
for Young Ladies

Book 1 of 3

By Marcy Shoberg

Not Prey:
Facing the 7 People-Dangers for Young Ladies Book 1

ISBN-13: 978-1-948972-00-0
ISBN-10: 1-948972-00-X

MKS Publishers
www.marcyshoberg.com

Three-Book Contents

In Book 2 for **Facing the 7 People-Dangers 102**

In Book 3 for **Facing the 7 People-Dangers 201/202**

Welcome Back

Graduation Day

Acknowledgements and Further Resources

Welcome to Class

Thanks for studying interpersonal dangers (dangers between people) with me. Knowing about the seven people-dangers will help you recognize bad situations earlier, when you have more and simpler options for keeping yourself safe. In these books, you will learn strategies and skills you may someday use against a seriously dangerous person. And, you'll be pleasantly surprised to find many of these strategies and skills help you deal with not-so-dangerous people such as peculiar roommates, bothersome parents, and grumpy boyfriends.

We tend to classify things when studying them. When you were first learning language, maybe someone showed you a little poodle and told you it was a *dog*. You thought you understood, until you were introduced to a German Shepard or Rottweiler *dog*. Eventually, you figured out there are different kinds of dogs. Now, you can instantly recognize any breed as a type of dog.

If your kindergarten teacher asked you to draw a dog, you could. But, what if they asked you to draw a dangerous person? Most kids, I think, would draw a tough-looking man with a mask or with a trench coat and hat. But, as you may know, the concept of *dangerous person* is more complicated than that of dog.

Here you are, on the verge of adulthood, needing to be prepared to protect yourself in the world. What do you do about rapists, bullies, abductors, mass-shooters, stalkers, robbers, and other bad-guys? First, understand practically no one walks around clearly identifiable as dangerous. Obviously, *bad-guys* (or *bad-gals*, for females) want to blend in, seeming normal. Reading this book will help you notice signs of a potentially dangerous person.

Bad-guy isn't actually a very helpful concept. Most of the people you will ever need to protect yourself from are just regular people considering doing bad things. (We all sometimes consider doing bad things. If you don't believe me, you must not have brothers or sisters.) Your actions can often make a dangerous person decide against what they consider doing. Acknowledging that dangerous people are like ourselves helps us understand them. Understanding someone helps us deal with them.

You began studying protecting yourself from others right after you learned to use your senses and move your limbs. But, you probably never realized what you learned, or considered if it helps you deal with current threats in the best way. Some of you decided, as kids, being nice is always the best policy. Some of you, though, decided nice people get pushed around. It's time you all consider how *nice* it benefits you to be in different situations.

This book, number 1, introduces you to the seven people-dangers, teaches use of your natural self-defense tools (brain, voice, body), and outlines basics of dealing with people-in-general. In book 2, you'll study each people-danger separately, learning to best apply tools in specific situations. In book 3, you'll study using your self defense tools in the presence of complications such as weapons, additional people to protect, and sexual situations.

These three books are part of a series designed to help all ages better handle interpersonal danger. You can find the next volumes, along with *Facing the 7 People Dangers* books for preschoolers, elementary-age kids, guys, women, and others at marcyshoberg.com.

About the Author

I've purposefully studied protecting myself from others for over thirty years, since joining a taekwondo class at age 11. At first, I thought knowing how to use my body against someone grabbing or striking me was knowing how to protect myself. For the last fifteen years though, I've also studied the non-martial-arts self-defense industry. I've realized that, while martial arts is great fun and exercise, it doesn't teach people to deal with interpersonal danger. The classes ignore the thoughts and motivations of the people involved, the verbal exchanges that often come before physical danger, and all the many ways dangers can be stopped before they start.

Furthermore, martial arts moves are often too complicated for a person to use when adrenaline floods their body, as it will when they face danger. I highly recommend you supplement reading this book with a *self-defense seminar or workshop*. I've taken much *FAST* Defense training, a Model Mugging course, a RMCAT workshop, and an IMPACT Women's Basics course. Each taught me a lot and was much better training than others courses I've tried. (To be polite, I won't name the bad courses.)

For help finding a course for you, or if you're curious what the names of the above-mentioned self-defense classes mean, see marcyshoberg.com.

I've taught many self-defense courses, including a semester-long one at New Mexico State University. I've also written a self-defense newspaper column and studied what others write about self-defense. The main thing I've come to realize, that led me to writing this book series, is that we shouldn't think of self-defense as something we may someday need during an emergency—self-defense should be something we use every day to live boldly and enrich our relationships with others.

Yes, things you learn in this book will help you if you ever face an attacker in a dark alley. But, they will also help you deal with your mother, your brother, your lover, and everyone you ever work with.

Dealing with People

Just as self-defense skills help you interact with non-dangerous people, people-skills help you deal with people-danger. So, between self-defense chapters, these books will have brief people-skill topics titled *DWP* for *Dealing with People*.

When I realized I was clueless about dealing with people, I started to study the topic. I learned much from Brendon Burchard's *Life's Golden Ticket*, Dale Carnegie's *How to Win Friends & Influence People*, Doc Thompson's *Verbal Judo*, and other sources including work by Brian Tracy and a dog training manual. I'm no people-skill expert, but I'm very excited to share with you what I've learned.

One major realization I had is that dealing with people is like sport-fighting, which I also never excelled at. As a taekwondo competitor, I thought I should memorize exactly which move to throw in what situation. (When they *a*, you *b*. When they *c*, you *d*.) Nope. In sport-fighting, as with many sports, one should train a variety of strategies (counterattacks, offensive attacks, dodging movements). The theoretical best strategy for any moment depends on a player's strengths, their opponent's weaknesses, and how bodies are currently positioned.

But, since there isn't time to stop and think during a match, rather than seek the current best strategy, players should *wing i*t, keep doing what's working, and stop doing what isn't. In interacting with people, sometimes there is time to thoroughly consider strategy, like when you plan how to ask your boss for a raise. But, sometimes you can only wing it and adjust as you go, like when your roommate surprises you with a criticism.

Upcoming DWP topics squeezed between chapters will be concepts and strategies which have greatly improved my ability to deal with people, dangerous and not. If you're studying this book with a group, you might discuss each DWP when you discuss the chapter before it.

Disclaimer Section

This book is not intended for children. If you do not already have a basic understanding of the birds-and-bees, and of cuss-words, you should read a *7 People-Dangers* kids' book, instead. This three-book set includes descriptions of adult, violent situations so if you ever face one, you will not be too shocked to respond.

By continuing to read, you accept the risk that you may be made uncomfortable by some situations described. Also, by continuing to read, you certify that you either do not need a parents' permission to read violent stories with bad language or have obtained necessary permission.

Finally, understand no advice given is guaranteed to work in any particular situation and it is your responsibility alone to decide when to use which response, knowing that you may be injured or punished as a result of acting in self-defense, even if you do everything exactly by the book.

Chapter 1:

Starting Your Journey

I congratulate you for starting to study self-protection. This training is empowering, and often roller-coaster fun. Still, most young women never read a self-defense book or take a course. (Neither do most adult women, or most men.) I'm excited you are studying, and I hope you are, too.

I've noticed six reasons various young women have, for not studying self-defense. One, some don't know they can learn about protecting themselves. In fact, anyone can educate themselves to be better able to do anything. Two, some are too busy to make time for self-defense training. It's easy to decide to prepare for math tests and basketball games because we know exactly when they will happen. It's not so easy to make time to prepare for things we hope never happen. I'm sure, though, that you will be glad you did.

Three, some think someone else, such as their parent, their boyfriend, or the police, will always protect them. None of these people fit in your pocket, so you're smart to learn to protect yourself. Four, some feel they are too *girly* to learn to hurt someone if necessary. Humans are the only animals that ever believe protecting oneself is unladylike. A female guard dog is as good as a male, a female lion as dangerous as a male.

Five, some feel since nothing dangerous has happened to them before luck will always keep them safe. Or, maybe admitting they could face danger from another person is so scary for them they would rather stay in denial.

Yes, reading these books, or taking a course, will cause you to think about dangers you haven't before. We'll discuss dangers that happen to everyone, such as being insulted. We'll discuss dangers that happen to most people some time in their life, such as being held or hit. We'll discuss dangers that don't happen to most, but do happen to many young women, such as rape and robbery. And, we'll discuss dangers that are highly unlikely to happen to any particular woman, but do happen to some, such as being taken hostage. If you have previously enjoyed being in denial of such dangers, I think you'll be pleasantly surprised that facing your fears empowers you and enriches your life.

The sixth reason some never study self-defense is that they think they're well prepared because they're either good at running or at fighting. As you'll see in the next section, in chapter four, and many other places in these books, different situations require different responses. No one strategy will save you in all.

You somehow overcame all six of these barriers, and are now reading this book. Be proud of yourself!

You Can't Use the Same Answer for Every Question

There are four possible responses to any danger. The trick is to quickly decide which to apply in a certain situation, even while poop flies around so to speak. The possible responses are flee, fight, submit, and appear-to-submit while planning. Fleeing, as in running away, can be the best choice if there is a safe place to go and little motivation for the attacker to chase you. But, if the attacker is strongly motivated to harm you personally, you're with someone who can't run (grandma), there is no good place to go, or an attacker already has a grip on you, running is not an option.

In situations where running is a poor choice, fighting may be necessary. Please, before you read further, say aloud, "I am important enough to fight for." I heard of a three-question survey given to some large number of women. For question one, "What would you do if you were attacked?" the most common answer was, "I have no idea." For question two, "What would you do if you were with a friend who was attacked?" the most common answer was, "I'd try to help, somehow." For question three, "What would you do if you were with a child who was attacked?" most women indicated they were fully prepared to viciously fight the attacker. Men also often find it easier to summon the courage to protect someone other than themselves. We should all realize that, by being willing to protect ourselves, we do friends and family the favor of increasing our chances of being around them for a long time.

You may feel you couldn't bring yourself to hurt another person, even if you were in danger from them. That is normal. It is also normal if you gleefully fantasize about tearing the guts out of people who try to hurt you. Of course, an attitude somewhere between these extremes is safest. We should be as willing to hurt someone who attacks us as we would be willing to hurt someone who attacks a child we care for. But, we should recognize that it is legally and ethically wrong, and personally unsafe, to consider it our place to rid the world of bad-guys one gut-tearing opportunity at a time.

Fighting sometimes creates more problems than it solves. These problems include, but are not limited to, legal trouble and the fight's loser seeking revenge. Still, in some situations hitting a person can be your best option. Later chapters will cover how and when to hit someone. Times to submit to a dangerous person, and times you might appear-to-submit while waiting for a good chance to flee or fight, will also be discussed later.

Fighting Compared to Physical Self-Defense

Although, in the last section, I used the term *fighting* for *doing physical self-defense*, I avoid using it that way. To me, *fighting* is what people do when they *have a fight*. This implies all involved agree to try to harm each other.

In a *sport-fight*, such as a boxing or taekwondo competition, all participants follow the same rules, or they get penalties from a referee. And, since judges decide who wins, each fighter has some idea what the other is likely to do—the moves and strategies most likely to score. Sport-fighting can be a fun exercise activity, but it's not as related to self-defense as most people think. The most obvious differences are that sport-fighters use protective equipment and are relatively evenly matched in size and experience level (so spectators can wonder who will win). But, the most significant difference is in the mindset of the competitors—they've both mentally prepared for the event.

In a violent self-defense situation, the attacker has mentally prepared while the defender was unaware. But, the attacker generally expected no resistance from the defender (or they would have chosen a different victim). So, physical self-defense can be easier or harder than sport-fighting, but it's definitely different.

In unsupervised fights, like might happen in school hallways, each participant has their own set of *rules* in mind, and their own idea of what *scores*. One may be unwilling to use groin shots or eye-pokes, but the other isn't. One may be unwilling to pull out a weapon, but the other isn't. One may be trying to get the other to *give up* while the other's goal is to impress spectators. One may have mentally prepared for this fight for years, while the other only mentally prepared during the short verbal argument that preceded it.

While skills in this book could help a woman fight better, nobody really wins a fight like this. I hope this book helps you to stay out of *fights*, but to be victorious if attacked.

Your Feelings Matter

I don't know if you're the kind of woman who would not hurt a fly, or the kind who'd like to become a kick-boxing champion. I wish I could meet you and hear your thoughts. When I teach classes, we always take time to sit in a circle and share thoughts. It's amazing to see peoples' eyes open to points of view that first seemed foreign to them.

As you read this book, expect it to move you in different directions. There may be times where it makes you feel very vulnerable. You may find yourself temporarily looking at strangers as if you expect them to be dangerous. There may be times where this book makes you feel invincible and you find yourself sizing-up everyone you pass, half-hoping they are dangerous. Take time to feel your feelings and move through them. In the end, you will come out a more complete human, with knowledge of both the innate vulnerability and innate power of all women and men.

Each future chapter is followed by a list of suggested assignments and discussion questions. If you have the opportunity, it would be great if you could read this book as part of a group that discusses each chapter, and practices some of the moves together. You're also welcome to contact me, to share your thoughts, through marcyshoberg.com or to talk about the books on social media using #7peopledangersbooks.

DWP 1: Read Between the Lines

Once, I thought communication only meant to hear another person's words, put together their meanings, and respond with words that correctly explain my thoughts. Ha! It didn't take me too long to realize I also need to consider what the person *means* by words they use, even if it isn't what I would mean, and to use vocabulary they'll likely understand.

About thirty years after that point, I realized I was missing something very significant: People don't always mean what *you think* they say. Yes, sometimes people make truthful and correct statements. But, people also can lie, be wrong, joke, and use sarcasm. When lying, a person tells you something they know not to be true, to influence you in some way. When wrong, a person tells you something they currently believe, that either isn't true or isn't what they will later believe. When joking, a person speaks to entertain rather than to communicate, and means something different than the literal meaning of their words. Sarcasm is when a person says something nice, but means something mean.

Too, people can lie but, when caught, claim it was a joke. And, people can lie to themselves, which is basically the same as being wrong. As you hear a person's words, you've got to *read between the lines* for additional relevant information about why they speak them.

Do you *read between lines* well, or take all statements at *face value*?

Chapter 2:

Personal Protection Paradoxes

A paradox, as I'm using the term here, is something with elements which shouldn't match, yet is useful or true. Picture an ashtray made from a no-smoking sign. Or, think of the advertising slogan, "If your phone doesn't work, call us for help." Or, think of those booklets with the back of a page or two printed, "This page intentionally left blank."

One paradox related to our study is that, the greater your self-defense training and skill, the less likely you are to need to defend yourself. A person who knows how to fight, or to verbally deal with people-danger—or both—carries themselves differently. They have a *vibe* that inclines dangerous people to think twice before being dangerous to them. Does the fact that a person has prepared to do something they are now less likely to ever do mean they have wasted their time? I think not.

Our second self-protection paradox is trickier to understand, and can be upsetting. To say potential victims should study self-protection can seem to imply they are wrong for being attackable. However, obviously the attacker is the one who does wrong, not the victim. Many feel bullies need to be taught not to bully and rapists taught not to rape. To say potential victims need to be taught to act differently can be very unpopular. To some, promoting self-defense training is too much like *victim blaming*. (Victim blaming is, for example, telling a rape victim they caused the attack by the clothes they wore.)

But, it isn't as easy as it sounds to teach people not to do bad things. At the time a person does *wrong*, they are often under the influence of strong emotion, urges, alcohol, or drugs. Even if they once took a class in *how to be nice*, they wouldn't be thinking of their training when they most need it.

How would we even decide who needs to be taught how to be nice? How would we motivate the students to pay attention and make changes in their ways of thinking and acting? Can't threat of punishment make everyone be nice? Do bullies and rapists weigh the pros and cons of actions they consider?

These are important philosophical questions for society to consider. But, as a student of self-defense, please accept that you can't change other people, but you can change yourself. If you change yourself, you have a very good chance of changing how others treat you. This includes seriously dangerous people, bothersome people, and everyone else.

If you face danger from another person, they are wrong, not you. If you use knowledge and skills to get out of the danger (instead of just hoping they paid attention in *how to be nice class*), good for you.

Chapter Assignments and Questions for Discussion

1. What value do you see in a person preparing to protect themselves from interpersonal danger?

2.   How does your religion stand on the subject of self-defense?

3.   What are your thoughts about changing potential victims versus changing potentially dangerous people?

DWP 2: Strategic Speaking

Our last dealing with people topic was about reading between lines—understanding people say things for *reasons* and can lie, joke, or speak truthfully. If someone tells you, "Come here," you should wonder why they said it before you decide if you will go.

Additionally, as you speak, consider not only what you actually think, but also what you want your listener to think you think. Did I just say you might lie? Uh, yes. We all must find our own opinion of when lying is okay.

Can you tell someone they did a good job when you're actually not impressed? (In that case, "Good job!" means "I appreciate your effort and want you to feel good about it.") Can you yell, "Drop the knife!" when there isn't a knife you know of? (Here, "Drop the knife," means, "Everyone stare at this dangerous person!") Can you say, "I don't know if that's a good idea, let's talk about it," when you really mean, "You've got to listen while I try to talk you out of that stupid idea or we're all going to have big problems."?

Rather than always simply saying what you think, learn to speak the words most likely to have the effect you want.

When do you think it's okay to say something untrue?
Do you speak strategically, or just speak your mind?

Chapter 3:

The Seven People-Dangers
and Related Situations

When you decided to read this book, you may have been interested to learn to deal with one people-danger, such as bullying, robbery, or abduction. If so, I hope you're pleasantly surprised to find our topic broader than you expected. In these books, I try to give you skills to handle any situation in which you might unexpectedly find yourself wanting to stop physical or emotional danger or discomfort caused by another person.

Self-defense situations break into categories, as explained below. When you feel danger or discomfort because of another person, realizing the type of situation you face helps you find the quickest, safest way out. Book two has much more detail on each type.

A Quick Listing of the 7 People-Dangers

People-danger one I call *accidental confrontation*. Here, someone is mad at you for a good reason, a bad reason, or you-can't-figure-out-the-reason. Realize getting mad back might feel good but makes them madder. Instead of escalating the situation with body language, tone of voice, and word choice, deescalate it by staying calm. And, if you can't be sorry for what you did, at least be *sorry it upset them*. As they calm down, they will begin to think more clearly and you can work together to find a resolution.

People-danger two is the *territorial* self-defense situation. Here, a person is trying to make you go away. Either they want you to not be at *this place*, or to not be *near them*. The thing to realize here is that giving in to their wishes and leaving is a possible option, by definition. If going away wouldn't solve the problem, it's not a territorial situation: If it would, it is.

The other five people-dangers are *predatory*. In a predatory situation, the perpetrator knows what they want to do, and must choose who to *do it to*.

People-danger three is *robbery*, where a person chooses a victim they think will be easy and profitable to scare and take from. People-danger four is *bullying*, where a person chooses a target they think will be easy and enjoyable to harass. The first step to protecting yourself from these situations is to not seem a good choice of victim. More about this will be explained later. If it seems you might have been selected by a predator, the general rule is to stand up for yourself, loudly, until they change their mind. But, when a robbery has clearly started, risking physical harm over possessions is not recommended.

People-danger five is a *grab* or *strike* from an attacker who seemed to come from nowhere. Whether the attacker is mad at the victim, or choosing them to abduct or assault, doesn't matter because there isn't time to find out. Fighting would almost certainly be the best response in this situation.

In people-danger six, a predator uses *deceptive strategies* such as charm or trickery to bully, steal from, or abduct a victim. Recognizing the predator's strategies is the main defense here.

The final people-danger that we'll cover in book two is people-danger seven, *planned mass attacks such as terrorism*. Here, one or more persons decide to bully or steal from many people at once. We can all help protect each other from this type of danger.

Often, a situation of interpersonal danger easily falls into one of the above categories. Some though, can be difficult to classify. For example, a person may act mad or territorial when they are really bullying, which is predatory. Or, a confrontation can first seem predatory but, as a verbal exchange continues, something they say indicates that leaving would be a fine option, which makes it territorial. It is also possible for a situation to begin as one type, then change to another.

For now, just remember dealing with someone angry with you is different from dealing with someone trying to make you go away. And, both are different from dealing with someone who chooses you for a victim or target.

Dominance Contests

Another source of conflict, which will not be discussed much in these books, is the *dominance contest*. It is natural for social animals, including humans, to sometimes feel the need to decide who, in a group, is dominant over whom.

The previously mentioned seven people-dangers can happen between strangers *or* between non-strangers. But, dominance contests usually happen between members of a group, like a household or workplace. (I say *usually* because since *men* are known to sometimes have dominance contests with strangers, wishing to impress friends, I figure women might also.)

A dominance contest can feel like bullying. In simplest form, it starts with a challenge such as, "Are you looking at me?" If you choose to play this game, you would reply with either an insult or a similar challenge. Then, words would be exchanged and either someone backs down or a physical fight begins. As a result, you would be somewhat permanently labeled as either superior or inferior to the person who challenged you.

Human female dominance contests are often subtle, and may feel more like social bullying than physical self-defense situations. For example, a girl will try to tell her friend or female coworker who to date or what to wear, to enjoy controlling her. Or, they will try to make her embarrassed about her body, to feel powerful.

Participating in a dominance contest is risky. If it gets physical, you could be injured and/or face legal trouble. If you win, you are basically painting a target on your back such that anyone who wants to be the boss of your group feels they must challenge you and win. Backing down from a challenge, letting the other win, is a safe choice if challenged by a stranger. But, if challenged by someone you will see again, losing the challenge creates future problems.

Trying to win or choosing to lose dominance contests are not our only options. We can portray denial of the challenge, and try to seem too cool to play a dominance game. For example, the answer to, "Are you looking at me?" could be "I'm sorry, I think I need more coffee." And, the response to body shaming could be a smile that's impossible to interpret. This seeming failure to notice a dominance challenge is your safest way out of the situation.

Mindset Separates Self-Defense from other Fighting

Some situations are often confused with self-defense, but quite different. One is *combat*. Here, people are dangerous to each other because of their *job* (drug runner, law enforcement officer, gang member or military of opposing sides). In a combat situation, a person knows there is a chance of meeting their enemy so is somewhat mentally prepared.

Then, there is *sport-fighting* such as boxing, sport-karate, and sport-taekwondo. Here, participants know when to start and stop fighting, and what moves the other is likely to throw. So, they are very mentally prepared.

Then, there are *martial arts*. Some are designed to prepare for sport-fighting, some for duels popular long ago, some for battle-field-combat in pre-gun days. Many are designed for exercise, fun, and making money for the teachers. Asking which martial art is best for self-defense is like asking which brand of soda is healthiest: An answer could probably be found, but if you want health, drink water. Why take a martial arts class, if self-defense is what you want to learn?

Krav maga is an *integrated tactical combat and self-defense system*. That means it's an organized way to remember techniques which could be useful in combat or self-defense situations. Like in martial arts, krav maga students practice with *partners* (as opposed to attackers, opponents, or enemies). So, their mindset is one of teamwork to get moves right. Krav maga has great techniques, but for getting a person ready to fight for their life, it doesn't compare to armored-assailant self-defense training.

The essential difference between these other fighting situations and a *self-defense situation* is in the defender's thoughts. During an accidental confrontation self-defense situation, you might be thinking, "This person is totally unreasonable!" when you realize you're about to be hit. In a territorial situation, you might be thinking, "Who do they think they are to tell me where to be?" In a predatory situation, you would probably be thinking, "Is this really happening?" Beginning to use verbal or physical defense strategies from these mindsets is quite different from sport-fighting, martial arts, or combat.

Mindset is important because your primary tool for self-protection is your brain. Demeanor (your attitude plus your voice and body-language communication style) is your next-level tool for self-protection. Voice is your third, then weapon, then your body. As you'll learn in the upcoming chapters, to stay out of danger *and* trouble as best you can, use the highest level tool that will protect you in a given situation. For example, using your body when your voice could have protected you is taking unnecessary risk with your body and, in some situations, increasing your chances of getting in legal trouble.

Chapter Assignments and Questions for Discussion

4. Think about a time you felt like hitting someone. Would you classify the situation as accidental confrontation, predatory, territorial, dominance contest, or something else? What was your mindset?

5. Think of a time you faced someone who seemed dangerous to you. How would you classify the situation? What was your mindset?

6. How do dominance contests go with your crowd? How do you handle them?

DWP 3: Making Someone Like You

Often we try to make everyone like us, when we'd be better off trying to make the *right people* like us. Nevertheless, know that most people like you more the more you like them. They don't know this, they wouldn't admit it. But, if you make a person feel they are important, interesting, and valuable, they will subconsciously enjoy your presence and thus think they like you.

Do you think it's important that everyone like you?

How do you make a person feel important and interesting?

Chapter 4:

First Tool of Self-Protection, the Brain

Your primary tool for self-protection is your brain. If you can prevent or end a danger with the right decision at the right time, you save yourself physical and legal risk. Three aspects of using your brain for self-defense are your awareness level, the knowledge you have, and choices you make.

Awareness Level

Appropriate awareness level leads to noticing danger earlier. Earlier is better, so you have more options for dealing with the danger, and more time to choose one. A tool many self-defense teachers use to discuss awareness, called *the color code of awareness,* is explained below.

White is not aware enough, yellow is properly aware when there isn't any danger. Potential danger moves us to orange. Danger that requires action moves us to red—or to black if the action required is to hurt someone.

White awareness is a level of awareness that is too low. A person walking with earphones in both ears, playing a game on their phone, who could easily trip on a rock, step in a hole, or bang their head on a hanging sign, is in a white level of awareness. If a person, dangerous or not, approached someone in the white level of awareness, they could make physical contact before being noticed.

We go into the white level of awareness when we shouldn't for a few reasons. One is being distracted by internal dialog. If you're in public carrying on a conversation with yourself about someone who made you mad, things you need to do, or the show you watched yesterday, you're not as aware of your environment as you should be. Electronic devices can also put us into the white level of awareness. Somehow, we feel like answering a text is more urgent than what's happening right in front of us, even if we're driving. Crazy.

Sometimes, we *need* to go into the white level of awareness to momentarily focus on a task. (We don't need to answer texts while driving, however!) But, we must realize when we forget about our environment, we open ourselves to danger. I try to have a *five-second-check rule* when in the white level of awareness in public.

For example, if I were buckling a toddler into a car seat, I wouldn't spend more than five seconds focusing on that without listening or looking for things happening outside the car. Depending on the toddler, it might take several times back and forth between environment checks and focus on the straps to get the job done. Once, during such an environment check, I noticed a man looking at me intently. I stood up beside the car and said hello. It turned out he was no danger and wanted to chat about the logo on my jacket.

Or, if I was out on a date in a restaurant or bar, I wouldn't spend more than five seconds gazing into my date's eyes before glancing around the crowd and at the exits. Once, I had to explain that I was *not* checking out the doorman!

Yellow is the level of awareness for times without danger or immediate concern. In the yellow level of awareness, a person has their attention roughly equally divided among their thoughts and everything around them. So, they would probably notice anything that looks, sounds, smells—or in any way *feels*—unusual or potentially dangerous.

Anything noteworthy should move a person to *orange*. In the level of orange awareness, a person puts more, but not all, focus on one interesting thing. This interesting thing could be anything unusual such as the sight of a person running, the smell of smoke, or the sound of raised voices. A person should also move to the level of orange awareness when passing an object large enough they don't know what is on the other side (bush, van, building corner). At the time, curiosity about the other side of the obstruction should be slightly more important than the rest of their environment.

Besides the five-second-check-rule when in white awareness, another great awareness habit is the *one-check-around rule* when in orange awareness. If you move to orange awareness because you see a person running, look to see if there is a reason you should run, too. (But, if the person is running straight at you from steps away, skip orange and go to red awareness, taking action.) If you move to orange awareness because a stranger is approaching you in a parking lot, as if to make conversation, one-check-around might let you realize a moving car is currently more dangerous than the stranger, or that the person's goal is to distract you while their accomplice steals your purse.

After one-check-around, you would decide if the noteworthy thing, which moved you to orange awareness, requires you to act. If it doesn't, move back to yellow awareness and continue about your business. If you need to take action (dodge, run, duck, speak, yell, call 911, etc.), you move to *red* awareness and temporarily let all of your focus be on this one issue.

If you need to protect yourself by hurting someone else (using your body or an improvised or dedicated weapon), then you are moving to the level of *black* awareness. Skills you learn in this book can greatly increase your chances of dealing with danger without having to hurt anyone; but please once again say aloud, "I am worth fighting for."

After moving to red or black awareness and dealing with a danger, move back to orange, confirming the danger has passed while beginning to be aware of the rest of your environment. Finally move back to yellow awareness (equally aware of all parts of the environment) and go on about your business.

Remembering to bring your level of awareness back down after danger has passed is not easy. But, it would be a shame if a person were surprised to be grabbed as they passed a dark alley, successfully defended themselves by striking their attacker, then got hit by a car as they ran into the street.

I've heard a news report of two men walking towards each other while texting (in white awareness), bumping into each other, then arguing about it. They ended up physically fighting. The apparent winner forgot to move back to orange awareness and confirm the danger had passed. He turned to walk away (probably still totally pumped), and the apparent loser got up from the ground, pulled out a knife, and stabbed him in the back. I'm sorry I don't know the rest of the story.

Some people I know have one vaguely dangerous thing happen and the rest of their day is shot because they are stuck in a state of hypervigilance (being overly aware, looking for danger). Looking for danger is an awareness mistake because it causes us to narrow our focus and opens us to danger approaching from other sides. With practice and conscious effort, anyone can develop the skill of moving up and down the levels of awareness appropriately. Slow, deep breathing is an important part of moving down a level of awareness when it's time to do so.

The following personal story illustrates moving up and down the levels of awareness. I was walking in a neighborhood with a young child, in yellow awareness. As we approached a yard with many small dogs and a questionable fence, I moved to orange and mentioned to her that we should keep an eye on that fence to our right, in case any dogs busted out. As I did my one-check-around, I found a small dog aggressively approaching from the street on our left. I then moved to red awareness and positioned the child behind me, as compared to the loose dog. I yelled at it to go home, while I mentally reviewed what I teach in my *Defense Against a Dog* class, in case it was necessary for me to go to black. The dog let us keep walking, but followed us falling farther and farther behind. As it did so, I moved back to orange awareness, keeping an eye on the dog while also watching for cars and other dangers. When the dog was no longer following us, I moved back to yellow and we continued to our destination.

Internal Awareness

Before we move on, one more thing needs to be covered about awareness: internal awareness. Sometimes you know something is worthy of more attention not because it smells, looks, or sounds weird but because it gives you a weird feeling. A great book on the subject is *The Gift of Fear*, by Gavin de Becker.

Women call this internal alarm system *women's intuition*, men call it a *gut feeling*. Some people actually get a *feeling* in their gut when in a dangerous situation their conscious mind hasn't quite yet figured out. Others might get the feeling in their throat, or the back of their neck. Maybe this feeling is their guardian angel yelling at them. Most likely though, the person's subconscious mind has noticed that something looks, sounds, or smells weird, but not their conscious mind.

If you walk into a room and get a funny feeling about it, you are authorized to walk out. If you get onto an elevator with someone and get a funny feeling, you are authorized to get right back off. If someone says something to you that strikes you as odd, but you don't know why, you're better to trust your gut than the person. Learning when to listen to your conscious mind, when to listen to your emotions, and when to trust your gut, is a lifelong challenge we all face.

For more information, read *The Gift of Fear* where you'll find lots of great stories of people who knew something was wrong, but didn't know why, and saved themselves from danger. You'll also find stories of those who talked themselves out of trusting their gut, and regretted it.

Knowledge

Controlling your awareness level will help you notice danger at the earliest possible moment. Once danger is noticed, knowledge helps you choose how to respond. These books will increase your knowledge about people-danger. You've already learned a few important facts...

One, the best way to respond to someone angry with you is to use empathy to help them calm down. Two, one good way to deal with a person trying to make you leave is to go away. Three, a predator wanting to rob someone will look for someone with valuables who is easy to take by surprise. Four, a bully chooses the easiest and most fun person to pick on. And, five, a predator who wants to abduct someone may appear friendly. The rest of this book, and the next two, will further expand your knowledge of people-danger and give you a wider range of self-defense options to choose from.

Besides this book, you can gain knowledge about dangers from many sources including news reports and movies. When you see a news report about a danger (on the internet, television, or elsewhere) don't waste energy worrying about it. Just consider how you might protect yourself from it, and file it in your subconscious mind under *things that might happen*.

Movies and television shows are an interesting self-defense topic. What a person learns from them entirely depends on which they watch. In some, women fail to protect themselves and are either rescued by a man or victimized. In others, men and women protect themselves equally but quite unrealistically with techniques that took multiple tries for the stunt-people to get right, even though they are martial arts experts and their attackers wanted them to get it right. But, in a few shows, realistic men and women realistically protect themselves from danger. Keep an eye out for realistic dangers and good (or bad) self-defense actions as you watch movies and television.

Choices

Notice too, that your choices in life lead to greater or lesser risk of danger. Choices of whom you associate with, where you go, what you wear, and what you say to people can either increase or decrease your chances of facing danger. This is not to say that you need to always make the safest choice: That is for you to decide. But, when making a less-safe choice, you should realize and increase your awareness accordingly.

If you're going to date a tough-guy, you need to quickly learn strategies for calming him. If you're going for an exercise run in a secluded place, you need to take steps to prepare to deal with danger alone. If you park next to a van, you need to watch for signs of activity near its doors as you enter and exit your vehicle and be mentally prepared to fight if you are grabbed. If you're going to wear a short, tight skirt, you need to realize it might lead to unwanted male attention (not from serial rapists though, as they are not known to choose victims based on clothing) and you need to commit to letting the skirt tear if you need to knee anyone in the groin.

Besides the five-second-check rule for white awareness, and the one-check-around rule for orange awareness, I suggest you build another awareness habit I call the *three-most-likely-dangers-list*. As you prepare to go out, consider the three dangers you are most likely to face including, but not limited to, dangers from other people. For example, if you're taking a walk in your neighborhood, your three most likely dangers might be loose dogs, cars, and falling. But, maybe you have good balance but a bad neighborhood and your three most likely dangers are loose dogs, cars, and your neighbors.

If you're going out to a house-party, your three most likely dangers might be getting in a fight, drinking too much to safely drive, and having your car broken into. If you're underage though, your three most likely dangers might be getting in trouble, unwanted male attention, and drinking too much to safely drive home. The three-most-likely-dangers-list would be different for each individual and in each situation.

This is not to say that dangers not on your list cannot suddenly arise: Stay in yellow awareness, being likely to notice any danger as much as one on your list. I'm simply suggesting you pull some knowledge about dealing with your three most likely dangers to the front of your brain, and consider how your choices increase or decrease your risk of these dangers.

When you first make three-most-likely-dangers-lists you may feel stress because you consider dangers you hadn't before. Or, you may feel silly whenever you decide to change a plan based on something that probably won't happen but would be a disaster if it did. Eventually though, you'll decide how much risk is right for you and make it a habit. Then, it can be as natural as always checking to be sure you have your keys before you lock a door, or checking for food on your face when you pass a mirror.

Chapter Assignments and Questions for Discussion

7. Develop a habit of using the five-second-check rule when you're focused on a task while in public, and thus stuck in white awareness.

8. Develop a habit of using the one-check-around rule when something catches your attention and you are therefore moving to orange awareness. The way it fits with the rest of what's happening may be important information.

9. Practice consciously bringing your level of awareness back down after a stressful event. In *FAST* Defense, we breathe in through the nose twice and out through the mouth once while doing this.

10. Have you ever received a message from your intuition? What was it and how did it help you?

11. Let media reports of dangers educate you about possible situations people can face, but don't let them turn you into a worrier. What are some recent dangers being talked about by your local news?

12. Watch fictional dangerous situations with a critical eye, considering if the danger is realistic and if you agree with the characters' choices. What do you consider an example of a show where characters use good self-defense? bad?

13. Develop a habit of making three-most-likely-dangers-lists as you go about your daily activities. Be in yellow aware-ness so you would notice other dangers, but consider how your choices relate to your three most likely ones.

DWP 4: Avoid Triggers/Buttons

Most people are sensitive about a few things. Some call these the person's *trigger*, others call it a *button* as in, "Ignore him, he's just trying to push your buttons." For some people, calling them bro, dude, or sport, is an insult. For some, talking about their weight, questioning their honesty, or pitying them, puts them in a fighting mood.

We'll visit this topic again, in multiple self-defense chapters. For now, I just want to point out two things.

One, if you've noticed the triggers or buttons of people you spend time with, avoid hitting them during arguments or discussions. Once you've hit one, they don't care to understand your point, only to argue. (This is also why you don't list bad things they did before.)

Two, every time you notice a button of yours, which someone might use to pick a fight with you, commit to disconnecting it. Your goal is to eventually have zero ways someone can make you unable to decide how, in your best interest, to respond.

To disconnect a button, first identify it and explain it to yourself. ("I notice I get triggered when....") Then, decide that whenever you feel the button being pushed, you will take deep breaths and think before speaking. In some situations, you may decide to ignore the offending statement or action; but in others you may decide to make a joke or show you are offended. The point is you will *decide* rather than react.

Do you tend to push other peoples' buttons when angry?

Start keeping a list of triggers/buttons you see in yourself.

Chapter 5:

Second Tool of Self-Protection, Demeanor

Your next line of defense, after your brain, is the way you portray yourself. This includes body language, choice of words, and tone of voice. Think back to the chapter on different self-defense situations. When I first realized that stuff, I wondered whether accidental confrontation, territorial, predatory, or dominance contest situations were most likely. Finally, it hit me that the likelihood would be different for each individual, based on their personality.

Some people are so constantly friendly and pleasant it's about impossible to get mad at them or get them into a dominance contest. But, these same people could be easier victims of a predator because they would be slow to be suspicious or to raise their voice. Other people are very quick to anger. These people would be unlikely to be chosen by a predator (except a bully who enjoys irritating them), but have a greater chance of experiencing the other situations.

We can affect how we seem to others, showing different aspects of ourselves at different times, for different reasons. Remember the Benjamin Franklin quote, "Moderation in all things—including moderation." It's not a question of should I be this or that (nice or mean, flexible or rigid, trusting or suspicious), but of how much this or that should I be *in this situation*. The answer is usually near the middle, between *this and that*. Neither be too quiet, wimpy and passive, nor too in-your-face and aggressive. Be near the middle of the scale—assertive.

Excessively passive people give off a vibe that says, "I'm a good victim." It's the way they hold their eyes, shoulders, and hands, and how they walk. If this is you, force yourself to keep your shoulders up, your hands moving freely, and to look at people's faces in a pleasant way. If you find looking at another person's eyes difficult, know that it's just as effective to look at their eyebrows or nose. I was over age 20 before I could comfortably look people in the eye. I don't know why this was hard for me, but I know I was a favorite target for school bullies.

Excessively aggressive people give off a vibe that says, "If you're looking for a fight, here I am." Again, this is in the way they hold their eyes, shoulders, and hands, and the way they walk. Many with this problem are secretly insecure and fear being victimized. It's as if they tried to fix their *victim vibe*, but went overboard. If you have this problem, try putting your hands together, as if praying, while you talk to a person. And, also look at people's eyebrows or noses instead of their eyes.

If a passive person has a complaint against another, they might not even tell them. ("Oh no, this isn't what I ordered and I don't like it. I'll just go hungry.") Or, they might explain the problem as if it isn't really a problem, and let the other person take advantage of them. ("I guess maybe I did say over-easy, even though I never remember ordering anything but scrambled eggs in my entire life. Never mind.") An assertive person would nicely explain the problem as many times as necessary to get what they need. ("I'm sorry to be trouble, but this isn't what I ordered. What can we do about it?") An aggressive person would make the other defensive with the way they explain the problem, not realizing defensive people are rarely in a mood to be helpful. (Do you have a hearing problem or are you just stupid? I ordered…).

A good waitress or waiter, of course, can deal with any of these types of people skillfully. But, you can't always count on others having good people skills. For various reasons and in various situations, you may someday need to communicate with a person who is not at all inclined to see your point of view or please you (creepy stranger, angry friend or lover, criminally insane person). In these situations, being too passive or too aggressive can quickly make a problem worse.

Consider television, movie, and book characters. List some that are too passive for their own good, too aggressive, and properly assertive. Now do the same with real people you know. Then, try it while people-watching, maybe sitting at a mall. Who do you think looks easy to intimidate and who easy to pick a fight with? Finally, consider yourself and whether you tend more to be too passive for your own good or too aggressive.

Tone of Voice

Next, let's consider tone of voice. We'll do an exercise with the simple statement, "Leave me alone." I'm now going to ask you to repeat those words in different ways. By modifying your tone of voice, facial expression, and body language, you can make them mean quite a few different things. Please say, "Leave me alone," like you are terrified of the person you are talking to. Now, say the same words like you are disgusted by the person. Now, say it like you hate their guts. Now say them with an implied threat (like you seriously consider physically harming the person). Now, say the same words like you don't really mean them, but are playing around. Finally, say, "Leave me alone," like you simply and seriously mean the words and expect the directions to be followed.

I don't know if you were picturing the same scenes I was during the above exercise. Still, I think you now understand how you say words can be more important than what you say. Soon, we'll discuss what to say—and how to say it—for different situations.

At this point, I only wish you to understand the following. One, if you seem scared, dangerous people can be encouraged. Two, if you seem insulting or threatening, dangerous or mad people will likely be in a mood to insult or threaten you *back* (now or in a later revenge incident). Three, you can control your tone of voice. And four, facial expressions and body language can change the meanings of words.

Chapter Assignments and Questions for Discussion

14.   Consider fictional characters, deciding if they are especially passive, especially aggressive, or near the middle of the scale at assertive.

15.   Do the same for people you know and for yourself.

16.   Watch a group of strangers and decide who looks easy to pick a fight with or easy to intimidate.

17.   If you tend to be overly passive or overly aggressive, take steps to change your body language and patterns of eye contact.

18. Learn to control your tone of voice by giving different meanings to the statement, "Leave me alone." For more practice, of course, you could try it with other statements like, "Please stop," "It's time for you to leave," and, "Pizza is my favorite food."

DWP 5: People are not Machines

If you read between lines, and use strategy when you speak, will communication always go your way? Nope. You can do your best to calm an angry person then find them more inflamed. You can carefully choose words and actions to make a someone understand your point but fail.

Nothing you say or do to someone will get a totally predictable result because people are not machines. Machines always give the same output to a particular input, in theory.

Different people respond differently to the same treatment, and a person might respond differently at different times. If you give a person a look that reminds them of their mother, the reaction you get can depend on what they think of her. Slang or foul language make some enjoy your company but others take offense. Ask someone for a favor before they've had morning coffee and get your head bit off; ask the same thing at lunch, they'll be glad to help. Your words and actions interact with thoughts already in someone's brain and their habits and past experiences, in ways not easy to predict.

It's natural to think other people think like we think. But, no two people on the planet have the exact same way of thinking. To predict how someone will respond to something you do or say, it's not pointless to consider how you would respond in that situation. But, you may make a better prediction if you consider how you would respond if you had the same life experiences, beliefs, attitudes, and opinions they do.

Have you been guilty of expecting people to be machines?

Do you think normal people always think like you about everything?

Chapter 6:

Third Tool of Self-Protection, Voice

Interpersonal violence always begins with a *thought*—inside someone's mind. Usually, it progresses to *words* before any physical contact. By protecting yourself during the word phase, you reduce your risk of physical injury and legal trouble. So, if your awareness, choices, and demeanor have failed to keep you from danger, your next tool to apply is *voice*.

I'm not just talking about using voice for defense against insults, a topic with its own chapter in book two. I'm talking about cases of life-threatening danger with an attacker intending to assault you or abduct you! If you sense danger, but have not yet been grabbed or struck, use your voice for defense.

A statistic we armored-assailant teachers use, first researched by Matt Thomas, says that 80% of assaults by men against women are successful just due to the attacker's verbal threats. That means that 80% of the time a man decides to attack a woman, he doesn't strike or grab her, but rather makes verbal threats and she is too scared to do anything but comply with his wishes.

To clarify, let me set a scene. You are walking along a secluded route that maybe wasn't such a good choice. A man jumps from behind a bush, blocking your path, and says, "Do what I say baby, and you won't get hurt." The statistic implies that 80% of women this happens to would freeze like a deer in headlights. But, not you. You will step back with your right foot, raise your palms in front of your chest and face (like giving your attacker a stop-sign) and yell, "Back off!"

More explanation on this *self-defense stance* is coming in the next chapter. Basically, it's a way to stand so you are prepared to hit, but don't look like you want to hit. Have your right foot a step behind your left, with hips facing forwards. Position your left hand a foot or so in front of your face, and your right hand a foot or so in front of your chest. Palms face out, towards the threat. In a red-alert situation, as you stand in a self-defense stance, you can use your voice to discourage your potential attacker. This works best if you are at least two paces away from the dangerous person, so your peripheral vision can see their entire body.

Why Verbal Defense Usually Works

To consider why verbal self-defense usually works, start with the man, mentioned earlier, who jumped out from behind the bush. If he wasn't very sure you were one of the 80% who would freeze and comply, he'd still be hiding, waiting for a better choice of victim. Now that he is surprised to realize attacking you will be more work than he expected, his plan is derailed and he must decide how to proceed. He might try to make bystanders think you are crazy, he might run away, or he might yell at you to leave him alone. In all of these cases, verbal defense has worked perfectly. However, he also might decide to make a more vicious threat. In that case, you will need to yell again, more forcefully.

Too, he might lunge for you. In that case, verbal defense did not completely work, but at least it gave you a chance to get into a good striking position.

Now, what if the danger isn't from some stranger looking to surprise and attack you, but someone you know who is angry enough to hit you? Ninety-eight percent of adults know it is wrong to just walk up and hit someone who makes them mad. Actually, I fabricated that statistic, but doesn't it sound right? We were all taught, in preschool, that it's wrong to hit someone who makes us mad. But, many of us later decided that, if you yell at a person until they threaten you or cuss, it's okay to break that rule. As you use your voice for self-defense, you will never threaten or cuss, so you will never give the angry person an excuse to feel justified in crossing that line and taking a swing. Not being able to justify it, most people won't do it.

Picture a friend or family member of yours, who is relatively easy to upset, and inclined to violence. Imagine you've upset them, and they are yelling at you, waving their arms, making fists, and turning red. You make a self-defense stance, but a little softer. When they take a breath, you say, "Help me understand the problem. I didn't mean to upset you." At least part of their brain will realize that, if they hit you, they are being a jerk. If instead you said, "Get outta my face, asshole," that same part of their brain might realize, if they relax now, they are being a wimp. Not wanting to be a wimp, they would choose between a harder verbal assault, and a physical assault.

Verbal self-defense will usually work because all humans are constantly deciding what to do. A person who thinks yelling at you, threatening you, or trying to trick you into trusting them is a good idea can begin to think otherwise due to your words and how you say them. If you respond to a dangerous person's words in a way they did not expect, whatever plan they had will need to be changed. This will take time. In most situations, you would adjust your verbal strategy based on how they respond to your words. In some few situations, as they consider their next action, you would run or strike.

Why Verbal Defense is So Difficult

There are several reasons verbal defense is difficult. Number three is that we rarely notice examples of good verbal defense. Our favorite movie characters don't say, "I appreciate that you are upset, and I think we can work together to resolve this in a way that benefits us all." They say, "Go ahead and make my day, punk." If you have ever had the experience of lying in bed thinking of what you should have said to some jerk, you are not alone. But, you are probably wrong. The snappiest retort is rarely the best verbal-defense choice.

The number two reason verbal defense is hard is that it often requires patience during a time of discomfort. We want an uncomfortable time (such as an argument or situation where we feel threatened) to end immediately. Our brains often incorrectly advise us to end the situation quickly by fighting back, trying to turn invisible, or giving in to what the dangerous person wants. However, our best course of action is usually to give the other person words to think about and time to think about them.

The number one reason verbal defense is hard—drumroll—is our bodies are programmed against it. As humans evolved, we developed an adrenaline response system which works as follows. One the brain decides there is danger. Two the brain orders the adrenal glands (internal body part near kidneys) to send out a shot of adrenaline. Three this adrenaline raises the heart rate, moves resources away from small muscles toward big muscles, and moves resources away from hearing and talking brain sections toward seeing and physical-action brain sections.

Our adrenaline response system prepares our bodies to fight, flee, or freeze. In situations of danger faced by other mammals, one of the three will be the best response. But, in many self-defense situations faced by humans, *communicating* is our best response. So, we need to develop the ability to force our thinking and talking brain parts to stay active even while adrenaline courses through our veins. (And to force the small muscles of our tongues to obey our commands even while adrenaline prepares our larger, running and fighting, muscles for action.)

This takes practice. Every heated verbal situation we ever participate in could be considered practice. But, there is a special kind of practice that develops this skill faster and better than any other: mock assailant self-defense class. In this training, participants have an opportunity to face someone playing the role of an angry, threatening, or creepy person. This mock assailant will say scary things while staying far enough from the defender that striking is clearly not the right answer and communication must happen. The mock assailant will adjust the difficulty level of the exercise for each individual student. Another person, playing the role of coach, stays near the student and makes helpful suggestions.

After three to five experiences with this type of practice, most everyone finds it has become much easier to think and talk while threatened. Some people, at first, must overcome an urge to be too aggressive and threaten-back. Others must overcome an urge to be too passive, nice, and quiet. Some people must even first learn how to raise their voice.

I have a dare for you. Wherever you are while reading this book, yell "No!" Out loud. Right now. Ok, I double dare you. I triple dog double dare you to right now yell the one little word "no" in front of these people in the library, where your family or friends in the next room will hear, or wherever you are. Now.

Don't read this next paragraph if you didn't do it yet. Maybe you're thinking, "What will I tell everyone who asks why I just did that?" (Say, "This book made me do it. It's a good book, you should read it sometime.") Maybe you're afraid you'll be embarrassed after you yell. Maybe you just don't feel like expending that much energy at this moment. Maybe you're still trying to get up the nerve to yell, imagining what would happen if you did. Maybe you've already been thrown out of the library, I don't know.

My point is that raising one's voice is a skill some people need to learn. It involves deciding to use the lungs and larynx in a special way. It involves accepting risk of embarrassment. Sometimes, raising your voice can seem infinitely harder than enduring a bad situation. But, it is a skill a person can learn and benefit from. Imagine you saw a child about to stick their finger into a light socket, or a dog about to pee on your carpet. A shockingly loud yell of "no," like the one in my dare, is just the tool for the job.

There are many self-defense situations, too, where "No!" is a great choice. But, next I'm going to cover some sample statements that I've found much use for in mock-assailant self-defense training. I like to call them *red-alert statements*. For each, I'll set a scene that I hope will help the concept stick in your mind. Still, this is not a substitute for taking a class of this type yourself. Please repeat the title of each section aloud, before and after reading the section.

"I know how you feel, that would make me mad, too."

You have just parked your car at a shopping center and, as you exit the vehicle, an angry person comes running to you and stops two steps away. Waving a fist at you, they say, "Are you blind or some shit? You almost ran me over! What the fuck is wrong with you, bitch?"

You make a soft version of the self-defense stance mentioned earlier, palms facing them, about the level of your chin. And, with a sympathetic facial expression, slightly quieter than their voice, say, "I know how you feel, that would make me mad, too." They, slightly more calm, reply, "You're damn right I'm mad. I could've been killed back there."

You've now turned a potential fight into an uncomfortable discussion. Whether you did almost hit them or they are mistaken, hasn't mattered up to this point. Your next statement might be, "I'm sorry, I should have been more careful," or, "I'm sorry that happened to you, I wonder if it could have been a different car that looked like mine. But, do you want me to call the police to make a report?" Things proceed in a calming direction from there, if you play your cards right.

"I didn't mean to bother you, I'll go."

You are walking down a neighborhood sidewalk when a shady character steps in your path and says, "What do you think you're doing here?" Not quite sure what's happening, you reply, "Pardon me?"

Glaring and pointing a menacing finger at you, they say, "Your ugly ass is not welcome here, stupid." Before they finished the statement, you've made a self-defense stance with your left hand high enough to cover part of your face. Processing their words, you realize this is a territorial situation and leaving is a fine option.

Now, while looking slightly nervous, so they will feel no need to intimidate you further, you announce, "I didn't mean to bother you, I'll go." You mentally review what is behind you and, feeling confident you can step back safely, you take several steps back, bringing your hands down an inch each time. After mumbling, "That's right, pussy," they stop paying attention to you.

Finally, you turn and walk back the way you came, occasionally glancing over your shoulder wondering if you've ever seen that person before in your life. But, you finally realize it doesn't matter if you have or haven't, and you can now go on about your business, taking a different route.

"Back Off"

As you wait for your ride outside a shopping center, a normal seeming man approaches. He says, "It's hot out here today." Since he is keeping a respectful distance of two arms lengths from you, you don't think there is any danger and reply, "Yup."

Then though, he continues with, "You're the hottest thing I've seen in a long time and I might just pull you over into those bushes and have my way with you." Before he's done speaking, you've made a self-defense stance and yelled "BACK OFF."

He takes a step back and, looking hurt, says, "Geez, I was only kidding, bitch. What's up your ass?" You repeat, exactly as before, "BACK OFF." He walks away, laughing.

"That's inappropriate, I'm not interested."

Relaxing alone in a public park, you notice someone who seems to be behaving unusually, keeping their back towards you and glancing over their shoulder. You are embarrassed to realize you've just watched a man pee on a tree when the man starts to speak.

While walking towards you and zipping up his fly, the man says, "Since you think I'm such a good show, why don't you pay me? Five dollars." Still hoping things will stay calm, you say, "I'm sorry, I didn't realize what you were doing." But, since he continues to approach, you stand to make a self-defense stance with a serious face, hoping he will decide to leave you alone.

While not respecting your obvious wishes, he starts un-zipping again. He says, "No money? Give me a blowjob then." Already in your self-defense stance, you yell, "That's inappro-priate, I'm not interested," loudly enough that everyone else in the park wonders what's happening. He walks away grumbling about people who don't respect other people's privacy.

Discussion of the Above (No need to repeat that heading.)

I'd expect you to have questions and concerns after reading the sample scenarios above. First, you may be won-dering if that stuff really happens. Although I didn't take any of those stories from actual experiences, I designed them to help you prepare for unexpected situations that shock and confuse you. If you ever need to use red-alert statements, you may have a hard time believing what your eyes and ears tell you is happening.

Second, you may be wondering how I could dare type those bad words. I can because I need bad words to lose any power of shock they may have over you. Personally, I'm a fan of clean language. But, if there is any word a person can use that makes you so offended you can't think clearly, or any name anyone can call you that leaves you unable to respond, you've got a self-defense ability concern.

Third, you may have wanted to see our heroine win the fights. Instead, she ended them quickly and cleanly, sometimes even allowing the attacker to feel they won. Knowing how to choose to let a dangerous person leave feeling good about themselves, while still feeling good about yourself, is pivotal to self-protection ability.

Fourth, you may be wondering if you could react as bravely in real life as you did in the stories. Mostly. But, remember how our bodies are programed against using good verbal defense? In real life, you would feel uncertainty about how to respond. You might not even be sure you understand what the dangerous person says. You may slur your words or stutter. After it's over, you probably won't accurately remember what you said.

And, you won't immediately feel proud and safe. Adrenaline rushes cause surprising reactions. You may feel like puking or fighting or giving the next normal person you meet a big, juicy kiss. But, then you will confirm the danger has passed, check around your environment, take a few slow deep breaths and realize that, although you're not quite sure what just happened, you must have done a pretty good job of verbal defense because you are safe. I hope you someday take a mock-assailant class to get actual practice and coaching on use of voice as a tool for self-protection.

Finally, you may be wondering if it's really that easy to protect yourself from dangerous people. Is just yelling the right thing at the right time and knowing when to shut-up all there is to self-defense? Why did the dangerous people in our stories not continue their verbal attack or turn it physical? Usually it is that easy. The dangerous people in those stories had to constantly decide if they wanted to keep being a threat to you, or if they had better things to do. Your statements never made them feel like it would be easy to intimidate you, but also never made them feel embarrassed to walk away. But, it's not always that easy, which is why there is so much book left after this chapter.

Creating a Scene

Creating a scene is another important verbal defense concept. Here, rather than shouting or saying something *to* the attacker, you shout a statement *at* the attacker which is really intended for *everyone* within earshot. Possibilities include, "This man is assaulting me. He is [insert description of height and weight or of clothing]," and the old standby, "Fire!"

Creating a scene is a choice for any predatory situation, as long as there is reason to believe some not-involved people are close enough to hear you. It's probably not as good for a territorial situation as would be volunteering to leave. And, it's probably not as good for an accidental confrontation situation as would be showing empathy and helping the dangerous person calm down.

When you yell, "Fire!" or a description of someone, several things might happen. People may stare at you. (Remember, you chose to accept any embarrassment, thinking it was the best way to deal with this dangerous person.) The person may seriously question if they want to continue doing whatever they are doing. They may fear being arrested for their actions. People may approach, getting involved in a helpful way. Someone might call the police. The dangerous person may try to act like you are insane. The dangerous person may try to cover your mouth. (If so, it has probably become time for strikes.)

You're not sure exactly what will happen when you create a scene, but you're never sure exactly what will happen when you take any action. And, when you've realized a predatory attack is beginning, it can be just the thing to derail the attacker's plan, changing things in your favor.

Another method to create a scene is to yell, "Drop the knife!" regardless of the presence or absence of an actual knife. When I first heard of this, I thought it was crazy. As a martial arts trained person, I thought self-defense was all about honor and integrity. The idea of yelling a lie, to end a situation before physical contact began, boggled my mind. But, the statement is really starting to grow on me.

If you were in a public place, obviously in danger from someone, and yelled, "Drop the knife!" at the top of your voice, what do you think would happen? I think everyone would start filming the incident with their phones. That's going to make the attacker think twice. Note that yelling "Drop the gun!" is not a recommended way to create a scene because smart people would run away or draw their gun, if they have one.

So, there you are, putting gas in your car, when a scruffy-looking man walks up and asks if you could give him a few dollars because he needs to take his handicapped kids to visit his dying grandmother. You politely decline. He stands there and says nothing while you feel uncomfortable. He gets a look on his face, that you're not sure the meaning of, and begins to step towards you, reaching his right hand.

You slam into a self-defense stance and yell, "This man is assaulting me! White t-shirt! Red flannel! Green cap!" He instantly recoils, looking shocked. A family at another gas pump quickly jumps in their vehicle and locks their doors. An older couple who were about to go into the store look towards you, reaching under their shirts. The gas station attendant uses the intercom system to announce, "Lady, do you need me to call the police?"

The scruffy-looking man is speechless. He walks slowly away, down the street. "No thank you," you announce towards the clerk.

You may be wondering where the scruffy-looking man is going. Is he going to try his trick at another gas station? Is he going to tell his handicapped kids they will never get to see great-grandma? What really happened here? I introduced this level of uncertainty now because it is a fact you must accept. If you wait until danger is clear, it may be too late for your voice to get you out of it.

Possibly our man is walking away thinking, "If I'm ever going to raise the money I need, I've got to make some changes in my approach. Maybe I shouldn't ask women who are alone." If you misread a situation, and are rude to a person who was not dangerous, that is not a disaster. *Better safe than sorry* definitely applies to use of voice for self-defense.

"What's going on?" (Repeat it, not shouting but not friendly)

The last verbal defense concept I'd like you to learn now is the information gathering statement, "What's going on?" Your voice can be very useful when evaluating suspicious situations. The following is a real-life story.

My father was playing some complicated, high-dollar card game in a casino when he noticed a man, who was wearing three shirts and a funny hat, watching him. Being properly assertive, he says to the man, "What's happening?" The man replies that he is trying to learn the game. My father finds something about the man suspicious, but continues playing.

Later, my father is alone at a urinal in the men's bathroom when the same man enters, looks in the first stall, doesn't choose it, looks in the second stall (of two), and doesn't choose it either. My father finds this strange, but takes no action. Then, the man approaches as if to use the urinal next to my father's. I hear that is an odd choice, with other urinals available, as there were. My father finds this disconcerting. His adrenaline rises. Being taekwondo trained, I think his mind was half-expecting some referee to tell him when it was time to fight the man.

But, he gets punched from the side and his head hits a wall. The next thing he knows, he's on the ground receiving punches while holding the man's neck. Then, my father feels his wallet leave his back pocket. The man now runs from the room. My father struggles up and begins to give chase, trying to describe the man to people he passes, when he realizes the man has probably discarded his hat and top shirt by now.

The worst parts, in my father's opinion, were that the casino wouldn't let him continue to gamble with blood on his shirt, they wouldn't let him drive himself home, and the TV news called him *elderly*.

My father made an information gathering statement in the casino. But, he missed the opportunity to make another when the man checked the stalls for witnesses. And, he missed the opportunity to say, "What's going on?" or, "Step away from me!" when the man approached him. By the time the danger was physical, it was too late for him to protect himself because the first blow left him disoriented.

What if he had said something stern and loud to the man in the restroom? Would the man have said, "Shut up and let me rob you?" Or would he have decided against it? While we can't be sure, I think the man probably would have made some lie about why he was in the restroom then left.

Now, I'll remake the story with you as the lead character to illustrate use of the information gathering statement, "What's going on?" Some details will be changed.

So, there you are alone in the restroom fixing your hair when a woman you noticed as strange earlier walks in. She looks in all the stalls but doesn't choose one. Your conscious mind is not ready to admit that she is probably checking for witnesses, but you know something is strange. You turn away from the mirror and firmly say, "What's going on?" She replies, "I thought I lost my phone. You haven't seen it?" "Nope," you say, without taking your eyes off of her.

Is she telling the truth? Was she actually planning to rob you? If she was planning to rob you, will she go through with her plan? Well, she couldn't actually go through with the plan she already made because, in that plan, you weren't staring at her from a step away, you were distracted. So, will she quickly make a new plan involving robbing a person who is confidently staring at her? Probably not.

Chapter Assignments and Questions for Discussion

19.   Yell "No," out loud, as many times as you need for it to not seem like a ridiculously strange thing for you to do.

20.   Make up a story of a situation where you might use each of the red-alert statements mentioned in this chapter. Say the lines aloud as you mentally review the situation you create, so your voice will get a bit of practice. The statements were as follows.

   "I know how you feel, that would make me mad, too."

"I didn't mean to bother you, I'll go."

"Back off!"

"That's inappropriate, I'm not interested."

"Fire!"

"This man is assaulting me. He is [insert description]"

"Drop the knife!"

21. Make up a story of a situation where you might use the information gathering statement, "What's going on?"

DWP 6: Non-Answers and Dodging Questions

You may have a habit of honestly answering all questions, to the best of your ability. This can be helpful in school. But, there are many times it will not serve you. Remember, people don't always mean what they say. "Do you like it?" can mean, "I'm nervous about my completed project, calm me down." "What were you thinking?" can mean, "I'm mad about what you did." "Have I seen you somewhere before?" can mean, "I think you're pretty, will you come over and talk with me?" Read between the lines before you decide how to respond to a question.

Sometimes, you'll decide to answer it. Other times, you may give a non-answer, such as a grunt. Sometimes, you might respond with a question of your own like, "Why do you ask?" Other times, you might answer with a statement that changes the subject. To give a self-defense example related to the last chapter, if you have used the red alert statement, "Back off!" and your potential attacker replies with, "What if I don't?" do not answer the question: You want them uncertain what will happen if they attack. So, dodge the question replying, "Leave me alone."

Are you comfortable dodging a question when that's in your best interest?

Chapter 7:

Fourth Tool of Self-Protection, Improvised or Dedicated Weapon

If, in a situation of interpersonal violence, there is no opportunity to use your voice, you might choose to use a weapon, if available. Additionally, if a verbal defense situation changes such that the dangerous person is beginning to strike or grab you, it is probably time to move to this fourth-string tool, if available. That all sounds very simple, until you try to picture it happening.

I'll explain more soon; but first, I'll clarify what improvised and dedicated weapons are. A *dedicated* weapon is something which has use as a weapon for its main purpose, like a gun or pepper spray. An *improvised* weapon is something which has another purpose, but can be used as a weapon, like a rock or an umbrella. Classifying a knife is complicated, but I think you get the idea.

Dedicated Weapons

I'm not a big fan of dedicated weapons. It seems to me they mainly allow a person to avoid facing the possibility of danger by buying something then sticking it in a drawer. I'm not saying *you* shouldn't have one: You must decide for yourself. Consider laws where you live, and risks associated with owning it. What is the chance of someone in *your* household using it against another in anger or by accident? Every woman might have a different answer to that question.

Imagine you carry pepper spray. Please reread the voice-defense situations in the last chapter, deciding how and when, in each, you would use it.

Don't read this paragraph if you haven't done what I asked in the last! Personally, in the accidental confrontation situation, use of pepper spray just doesn't seem *right*, to me. In the territorial situation, it might have worked or it might have made the situation worse. I have a friend who has worked security in bars. One night a big guy gave him a hard time: He used his spray. Then, the guy ripped off his shirt, wiped his face, and kept coming. A groin kick solved the problem.

In the "Back Off!" and "That's inappropriate…" situations, there was probably opportunity to pull pepper spray out of a pocket or purse. It would certainly have underscored your point, if you were holding the spray ready-for-action while using your voice. You would then be ready to spray, if necessary, wind permitting.

In the creating a scene and "What's going on?" situations, I don't see how a person would know when to draw their weapon. My father, by the way, had left his gun in his car since good-guys know it's illegal to take one into a casino.

If you get a dedicated weapon, do not neglect to be trained in its use. And, remember that it will do you no good if you can't get to it quickly. And, never forget owning a weapon is not a substitute for knowing how to use your brain, voice, and body to protect yourself from dangerous people.

I do know people who have been in dangerous situations where a weapon was the right tool for the job. Certainly, if someone is breaking in your front door and you can't run out the back door, a weapon would be nice to have. When seconds count, the cops are minutes away!

Improvised Weapons

The following is a story to help you understand improvised weapons. Say you're walking along with a big, heavy library book when a man jumps out from behind a bush and looks at you, threateningly. You step your right foot back and, instead of putting your palms towards him, you hold the book in both hands, so it's about a foot away from your face, just low enough that you can see over it easily. As you do this, you yell, "Back off!"

Notice that the way you hold the book makes it more of a barrier he must consider crossing than a direct threat to him. If the book was relatively light, you might hold it only in your right hand, using your left palm as explained before. Feel free use this book or another and stand up and try that right now.

Back to our story....

This man will most likely leave you alone. If, however, he moved to attack, you'd be ready to swing the book violently. Don't throw the book, because then you can only use it once. Swing the book, repeatedly striking him in the head—not that it matters much where you aim, if the book is heavy enough—yelling "No!" each time.

In my children's books, I explain that it is not wrong for a person to let a library book be damaged while using it to protect their body. But, I'll assume you know people are more important than things. What I'm not sure you know is how to swing a book while yelling "No!" So, please stand up and try it now. If you could actually hit something while you practice, like a bed or couch, that would be best.

Now, repeat our story above imagining that you have an umbrella or large flashlight, instead of a book. How would you hold it, and how would you swing it? If you can safely do so, please stand up and practice that as well. Then repeat everything as if you had a backpack or purse, instead.

Think through any objects that might be handy in your house, car, or places you often go. How would you use them to discourage a potential attacker, and how to strike?

If you had the opportunity to lift a chair between you and a dangerous person, I suggest you hold it by the seat, so they are seeing the ends of the four legs. You might then use your voice and wait to see what they do. Or, you might slowly walk forwards, towards an exit behind them, while using your voice, hoping they'll take the hint. (I hear that's what bar-security does.)

If you had a magazine in your hands when in danger, you might roll it so it becomes a sort of stick. If you had only something that was so light it wouldn't do any damage if swung, you could still throw it towards an attacker's eyes, possibly distracting them while you exit the scene or move in for a groin kick. An immovable object (tree or park trash can) could be an improvised weapon in some situations, as could a door that can be quickly opened or closed.

Keys are an interesting improvised weapon topic. Those who advise spreading four keys out between your fingers and making a fist are confusing self-defense with fighting. Sure, in a fist-fight, a pokey fist is an advantage. But, in any situation we've discussed so far, when would you recognize the danger and get your keys set up like that? Would a predator, seeing you had a *key-fist*, decide to leave you alone?

Probably. But, clearly an umbrella creates a more noticeable barrier. Many self-defense teachers instead advise walking with your keys in your hand with the next key you will use positioned where you could both stab with it *and* use it to get into your door quickly.

Conclusion

Usually, your brain and demeanor can keep you out of danger from other people. If not, using your voice well will almost always make you safe. Still, *if*, as you move to orange or red awareness of a potentially dangerous person, *if* there is anything already in your hands or easy for you to grab, know that it could be used, along with your body language and voice, to discourage the dangerous person from continuing.

If you've got an improvised or dedicated weapon ready, and a physical attack is imminent (*totally* starting to happen) it's almost always safer to use the weapon than to drop it and use your body as a weapon.

I can only think of a few possible situations where you might be smart to drop your weapon and use your arms and legs instead. One is if you have pepper spray ready but the wind is blowing the wrong direction. Another is if you have a potentially lethal weapon ready and you are under attack from someone the law wouldn't clearly recognize as dangerous to you. (Regardless of your age, I believe the law would recognize a male teenager as a potential danger to you. But, a physically fit adult woman might have trouble justifying shooting an unarmed teenage female attacker.) The last one is if you have a handgun in your hand when facing danger, but don't have a clue how to operate it or know it's not loaded. Rather than drop the gun though, you might swing it as an improvised weapon.

Chapter Assignments and Questions for Discussion

22. If you own a dedicated weapon or have one in your household, take a class on how to use it.

23. Consider improvised weapons found in your house, car, and other places you often go. Practice holding a few of them in front of you while using verbal defense and swinging them while yelling "No!"

DWP 7: Making Someone Agree with You

You actually can't make someone agree with you. In the words of Dale Carnegie, author of *How to Win Friends and Influence People*, "Those convinced against their will are of the same opinion still." But, there are a couple of tricks that can help.

First, don't tell someone they are wrong because they will stop listening due to defensiveness. You might even wait until their stupid opinion is all the way out of their mouth then say, "Yep. Also…" and give your smart opinion, as if it adds to their stupid one rather than contradicts it. Or, you could act as if you don't disagree with them, but others do. This would go like, "Huh. What would you say about people who think…?" Then, they will think about that point of view and might decide, on their own, to change theirs. Or, they might get upset and ask, "Why, is that what you think?" Dodge the question, as explained in DWP 6.

Find a chance to practice one of these strategies today.

Chapter 8:

Last Tool of Self Protection, Your Body

This chapter is an introduction to using body parts as weapons. Remember though, to avoid danger and trouble, use the highest-level tool possible. If there is a decision you can make, or a way you can portray yourself which avoids a need to use voice for self-defense, do it. If there is a way to use your voice instead of a weapon or your body, do it.

If though, your brain, demeanor, and voice have failed to keep you out of danger, and use of a dedicated or improvised weapon is impossible or inappropriate, you may be in a situation where you need to use your body as a self-defense tool. In books two and three, we'll talk about situations for submitting, and for appearing-to-submit-while-planning. Too, there are situations where fleeing would be best, but now you'll learn about fighting.

Obviously, reading about striking someone isn't likely to make you proficient. I hope you will someday take an armored-assailant self-defense class and get actual practice striking a mock-attacker. At the least, practice the techniques in this chapter in the air, imagining hitting a real person. Remember though, I can't see if you are doing the moves correctly or safely, so you can't blame me if you knock over your television set or trip and fall, okay? And, if you ever need to hit someone to protect yourself, I can't guarantee it will go well for you. And, if you decide to hit someone when you could have used a higher-level self-protection tool, you do so at your own risk. Only continue reading if you take full responsibility for your future use of the information!

All of that disclaimer-junk being said, please repeat again, "I am important enough to fight for." Someday, you might find yourself in a situation where attempting to use a strike you've only read about is safer than not attempting to use it. That's when you'll know it's time to hurt someone, and you will give it all you have. Never hit people in anger. But, when strikes come from a place of intense fear, they are usually the right choice and usually stronger than you could ever imagine.

Standing Self-Defense Stance

This position was covered earlier, but we'll now go into more detail. Stand with your left foot a step ahead of your right, both feet pointing basically forwards, but at an angle comfortable for you. Make the step a little bigger than your normal walking step. From this position, you should be able to strongly bring your right thigh straight up between an attacker's legs, if they were right in front of you.

Raise your hands in front of your body, elbows down and at ninety-degree angles, palms facing away from you. Imagine a person standing two paces in front of you. To them, your hands should clearly indicate that you are asking them to not come any closer. In a situation of potential but unclear danger, just making this body-language request, and seeing how they respond, helps you evaluate the situation.

Before reading this book, you may have thought a fighting stance would be useful for self-defense. Please now position yourself as a boxer stands and think about the message it sends. This message is, "If you want to fight, let's get it on."

Now, straighten your legs and turn them forwards while facing your palms out, so you are back in our standing self-defense stance. There are three messages it sends: I don't want you to come closer; there is a barrier of my hands you must pass to attack me; consider if you want to find out what I might do with my hands. What you might do with your hands, by the way, is send five fingers into each eyeball. But, we'll get to that shortly.

Please now check the angle of your elbows (ninety degrees). Ensure your hands are neither too close to, nor too far from, your body and face. If they are, you wouldn't throw a very powerful strike. Now, raise your left hand higher until it would obstruct an attacker's view of your face, but not so high it blocks your view of theirs. Your potential attacker is probably fixated on your face as the object of their hatred or desire and, by blocking their view, you make it just a little easier for them to decide to leave you alone.

Later, I'll explain other reasons I recommend this high position for the left hand, and why I recommend left-handed people do the standing self-defense stance this same way. I'll also cover *ground* and *deceitful* self-defense stances.

As you look at your imaginary attacker, mainly note their right shoulder, watching for signs of movement. Your peripheral vision should be able to note movement by any part of their body. But, since most people are right handed, your first indication that they are initiating physical contact and you have no choice but to strike will usually come from their right shoulder.

Now, let's study the two strikes I've already mentioned in this chapter: fingers-to-eyes and thigh-to-groin. These are the first self-defense strikes a person should learn because they are most likely good choices in a fight-for-your-life situation. These are not strikes to use when playing around.

If it surprises you these are the best strikes for high-danger situations, consider sport-fighting. Most moves used in any sport-fight are whichever are most likely to score with the judges. For taekwondo it's round kicks; for boxing it's face punches. But, what two moves result in a referee calling a time-out in every sport-fight I can think of? Eye pokes and groin shots! If you're in fear for your life, do you want to out-score your attacker or cause them to need a time-out?

Fingers-to-Eyes

Imagine you are in a standing self-defense stance, facing a dangerous person. Although you have used good verbal defense, they begin to step towards you with their arms moving as if to wrap around your upper body. You squeeze the five finger-tips of each hand into tight circles, making two beak-hands, and move them forwards, striking your attacker in both eyes at once while yelling "No!" Then, you bend your elbows and repeat, then repeat again. Please stand and practice this a few times, slowly, before you read the next paragraph. (Saying "no," instead of yelling, is fine during *slow* practice.)

Now, I'll answer questions I suspect some readers have. There is nothing magical about the number three: Do as many eye strikes as necessary to make yourself safe, or to make it obviously time for a thigh-to-groin, instead. The reason all five fingers should be put together is so the pinky can't hit a cheek-bone by itself. You hit both eyes at once so the attacker is unlikely to turn their head and take the hit on the side. There are other types of eye strikes, coming in later chapters.

If you are not athletic, hit as hard as you can. If you are athletic, just hit hard. (For eye strikes, a higher level of power is not better, enough is enough.) We are not trying to damage our attacker's eyes. It's fine if we damage them; but, our goal is to cause our attacker to lean back and bring their hands towards their face. This stops them from reaching and makes it easier to hit them in the groin.

Other questions you might have at this point are, "Would that work?" and, "What happens next?" I'll answer these together, after I ask you one question—Did you notice when the strike happened? If you need, reread the first paragraph of this section to find the answer.

The first strike happened as the attacker made a motion to contact you! If you throw eye strikes, at this time, with serious intention to hit the attacker in both eyes, it will change your situation in one of the following ways, all of which are improvements. The attacker may leave, or scream in pain. (If running makes sense in the situation, flee then.) They might lean their head away from you, covering their eyes with their hands: It's not that they would choose to do this, rather its an instinctive reaction. (Keep striking or flee, depending on other factors,) Finally, they may grab your wrists as you strike, or wrap their arms around you while furiously blinking. In these cases, it is time for thigh-to-groin, explained soon.

Please stand up and, from a self-defense stance, perform another set of three eye strikes. All five fingers in a little circle. Both hands moving at once. Yelling "No!" each time. Go ahead.

Finally, I will answer the big question…"Why do I have to yell 'No?' It seems hard to yell 'No' and I don't feel like it."

There are six main reasons I ask you to yell "No!" every time you throw any strike, in practice or in actual danger. One, it builds a habit of your stomach muscles tensing as you strike so whatever parts of your body touch the ground can push to help your striking parts hit harder. Two, it prevents breath holding, which may be your instinct in a dangerous physical situation, and would be bad. Three, it attracts exactly the attention you want—people wondering if there is a problem they should do something about. Four, it is a message to yourself that you will not stand by and be attacked: You will stop the danger. Five, it is a message to your attacker, with each strike, to consider ceasing their actions. (Not that they would decide to stop, but they may have a subconscious reaction to a yell of "No.")

Finally, number six, I want you to be the type of person who is comfortable yelling "No!" So, if you forgot to yell "No," when you just practiced eye strikes, please stand up and do them again.

Thigh-to-Groin

Imagine you are standing in a self-defense stance, beginning to throw strikes to the eyes, when your attacker grabs both of your wrists. The attacker is standing less than a full pace away, with their feet spread slightly apart. Bend your front leg (your left) into a partial squat, then use the strength of that leg to drive your hips forwards and upwards while you raise your right knee, which is bent at a ninety degree angle or more. The middle of your thigh slides from between their knees into their groin (*crotch, privates*), lifting them off of the ground, as you yell "No!" Your right foot lands a step ahead of your left, then returns behind you for another identical strike, and another.

Stand up and give it some slow practice now, please. Make sure your left leg is helping you hit hard. Confirm that the force of your strike knocks your imaginary attacker upwards, not backwards. Confirm you are contacting your imaginary attacker with the middle of your thigh, not your knee cap. Confirm your right foot lands a step in front of you, rather than back where it started. Finally, confirm that you are saying "No" with each strike.

Is it ethical to hit a man in the groin? That depends on the rules of the type of fight you are participating in. Wait, we're not talking about sport-fights. If you reasonably believe you are in serious physical danger from the man, yes. Is it effective to hit a woman in the groin? Effective enough.

Why are we using the mid-thigh upwards, instead of spearing with the knee cap? Well, it's harder to miss that way, as their legs guide your strike. And, it's harder for you to pull a thigh muscle, not that you should mind pulling a thigh muscle to save your life. But, mainly we do it that way because famous self-defense researcher Matt Thomas volunteered his own body for experiments to find out what type of groin strike would incapacitate a man quickest and most thoroughly and that's the one that won the contest. Thanks Matt!

Why step forwards, my right leg apparently prefers to land back where it started? The reason you land your foot back where it started is because you are not using your left (pushing) leg very well. In real-life, whether you step forwards or backwards after a thigh-to-groin depends on their weight compared to yours and the amount of friction your shoes get against the ground. But, in practice, always step forwards so your whole body is helping the strike hit harder. Please stand up and practice the thigh-to-groin again, harder. Remember to yell!

Isn't the man going to try to protect his groin? In a sport-fight which allows groin-shots, yes. In a sport-fight that doesn't, he will probably just wear a cup. Wait, we're not talking about sport fights. The man is thinking about grabbing you, or about striking you. If he thought fighting you would be hard work, he wouldn't have started the fight. So, most likely not.

Won't the man, hit in the groin, become angry and fight you harder? He might want to, but his knees are going to be trying to clench together, his stomach is going to be trying to roll him into a ball, and his pelvis is going to be trying to move away from you. This would also happen to a woman hit in the groin. Still, you won't wait to see what he does next. You will thigh him in the groin again and again until he falls, then thigh him in the head. We'll get back to this story in a couple of paragraphs.

The biggest danger while striking someone in the groin is having them fall forwards and accidentally head-butt you. As you practice thigh strikes, position your hands where they'd likely stop an incoming head-butt. Please stand and practice thigh-to-groin a few more times, thinking about your hands.

Is this situation (wrists grabbed from front after fingers-to-eyes) the only one in which to use thigh-to-groin? No. Others will be covered later, but realize you might someday be in a situation needing to fight for your life that isn't exactly like any we cover. You'd need to just look at your attacker, choose between eyes and groin, and go for it. In some positions, you might need to switch your feet or take a step before throwing thigh-to-groin. Or, you might be positioned where the left thigh is a better choice.

Please stand in a *reversed self-defense stance* and practice striking with your left thigh. Then try going forwards, alternating thighs: Right thigh, land it in front, partial squat, left thigh, land it in front, partial squat, right thigh...

Now, back to our story. You have, after thigh-to-groin, hit your partially fallen attacker with thigh-to-head. He will probably now fall to the ground, unconscious. If he does not, throw another thigh-to-head. You don't want to let him get to a standing position, because then you're starting over. If things go according to plan, after no more than a few thigh-to-head, he will be laying on the ground. Once your attacker falls completely to the ground, you will stop and watch him, in a standing self-defense stance. If he starts to get back up, you will thigh-to-head. If he seems unlikely to get up, you will take a good look at him, then look to see what else is happening around you, then decide where to go for help.

Similarly, if at any point your attacker had started running away from you, you would stop and watch, in a standing self-defense stance. After confirming he is no longer a danger to you, you'd look around. Maybe there are cars coming, helpful people coming, dangerous people coming—who knows?

Of course, not every physical self-defense situation would go exactly like our story. In some cases, after just one or two strikes, the attacker would run. In other cases, multiple eye strikes, multiple groin strikes, more eye strikes, more groin strikes, thighs to the head, and kicks from the ground could be needed. The story above is based on the series of strikes *FAST* Defense teachers have decided students should learn first: Fingers-to-eyes causes the attacker to lean back, thigh-to-groin cause them to fall to one knee, thigh-to-head causes them to fall unconscious.

Practicing these Strikes

You might expect me to tell you to do fifty repetitions of each strike once a week so you'll be able to use them when you need them. But, it's more complicated than that. When you need to use your body for self-defense, adrenaline causes you to feel very different from how you would feel while practicing, so the skills wouldn't transfer well. Based on work of other self-defense researchers, mainly Bill Kipp, I suggest the following.

Practice the strikes slowly, ten times a month, in an exaggerated fashion, while imagining using them against an actual human. (Be sure to imagine this actual human lifted off of the ground by the groin strikes.) If you focus on hitting hard, fast will come automatically. But, if you focus on hitting fast, you totally lose hard. Having trained yourself to strike in an exaggerated fashion, the adrenaline you feel during an actual situation will cause the strike to be both fast and hard.

I hope you someday take an armored-assailant course. There, a man (or very rarely a woman) would wear protective equipment on their head and groin and pretend to attack you. They would adjust the level of their attack to your level of ability, always challenging but never overwhelming you. In a class like this, you learn through the same process that creates post traumatic stress disorder: Since you are adrenalized when you practice striking, a similar adrenaline dump brings the knowledge back to you, even years later. It's post traumatic stress growth!

Even courses I highly recommend, that all descended from Matt Thomas' research, can differ somewhat. So, when you get a chance to take a course, don't be surprised if you're not taught exactly what I said above. There may be small changes in hand or hip position, for example. Or, they may teach things in a different order.

Other Strikes and Targets

I suspect readers with martial arts or fighting-sport knowledge are surprised at the simplicity of *fingers-to-eyes*, *thigh-to-groin*. Those get the best *bang for the buck*, so to speak. People can fight with broken ribs. Knees are easy to miss. Punches are hard to do effectively. Pressure points are practically impossible to hit when terrified, and just don't work on a small percentage of people.

Still, elbows, hammer-fists, groin-grabs, strikes with the shin, strikes with the heel of the foot, and strikes with the heel of the hand will come up in books two and three. In some situations, each would be the best choice.

Ethics and Legality

I'll end this chapter by emphasizing the importance of care in how you use striking knowledge and ability. I recommend you only strike a person to protect a body (yours or someone else's). Striking to protect property may be legal some places, and illegal others, but it's never a safe choice.

The legally and ethically safest choice is to only strike when danger is immediate (your attacker is beginning their attempt to contact you). Preemptive strikes will be discussed later, but know that deciding to harm someone you believe will later harm you is very risky. Still, so is letting your attacker get the first shot; so the general rule is to throw your strike when they start theirs.

You probably can't justify claiming striking someone was *self-defense* if things you said or did would reasonably be expected to cause them to attack you. (Don't participate in the escalation of the conflict.) So, always remember to use good people skills and verbal defense.

Stop striking a person when you have become safe. Earlier in the chapter, we considered you safe when your attacker runs away or stays completely on the ground. In actual practice, you must make your own decision based on the total situation. Know it's not uncommon for a person to rightfully strike in self-defense but get in trouble for continuing to strike after they ended the danger. These extra strikes could be done for revenge, or just because the person can't think clearly at the time. Doing so is wrong, and will likely get you in trouble.

I'm not a lawyer, but the following is my advice to you, supported by thoughts of other self-defense researchers, especially Peyton Quinn. If you ever need to talk to the police because you hit a person in self-defense, don't explain anything. Just say you don't feel well and want to be seen by medical personnel. Your memories of the situation can change drastically over the first day or so, as your adrenaline wears off.

Later, your lawyer can help you decide how to best explain what happened. Generally speaking, such an explanation would involve the following points. You were protecting someone's body, not property or feelings. You felt the danger was immediate, not *likely* at some future time. Threats or insults from you didn't help the fight get started. You made a reasonable decision about when you were safe and stopped striking at that time. Any explanation given to police, judges, or jury members should not include statements like, "I wasn't scared of that jerk!"

Chapter Assignments and Questions for Discussion

24.   Practice exaggerated eye strikes, starting from a self-defense stance, yelling "No!" Imagine contacting human eyes.

25. Practice exaggerated thigh strikes, starting from a self-defense stance, yelling "No!" Remember to imagine contacting a human groin as well as the head of a partially fallen human. Practice this on the right and left side, and with alternating legs.

26. Work through an entire *beginners' fight scene*, with an imaginary attacker: Start with a self-defense stance and use of voice for self-defense. Imagine a forward movement from your attacker, making you decide it's go-time. Use fingers-to-eyes, continue with thigh-to-groin and thigh-to-head. All must be done in an exaggerated fashion, while saying or yelling, "No." Do not rush from one strike to another. Remember: If you focus on hard, fast will come by itself. Finish by setting a self-defense stance and looking at your downed attacker, then looking completely around you, then pretending to decide where to go for help. Note that the absolute safest place to stand while evaluating a downed attacker is a pace away from the very top of their head. There, you can see them better than they can see you, and can hit them much quicker than they can hit you. If you have trouble imagining through this scene, check my website for video that might help.

DWP 8: Appearing to be a Good Listener

If you can actually be a good listener, that's best. A good listener can figure the best strategy to get someone to like them, agree with them, or do what they ask, because they can get a good idea what could put the person in the mood to do so. But, nobody's perfect and listening can be really difficult when your brain is screaming your opinion, or taking unrelated adventures.

To fake it, keep your eyes on the person speaking to you and occasionally nod, especially when you feel like shaking your head. If they are calm, hold your arms like theirs. If they are agitated though, appear very calm. When they tire of talking (or yelling), repeat back to them your best guess of their main points. ("Let me see if I've got it, you need me to…" or, "I hope I understand you correctly, you're mad because….") They'll probably correct your summary, which is when you really start to understand their point of view and can figure out how to proceed.

Find a chance to practice this today.

A.

Graduation Class

Welcome to our last class! (The last one until you start the next book, anyway.) I'm really glad you made it to the end, and I hope you feel empowered by what you've learned. You are no longer one of the many who deny they may ever face danger from another person, or think fists can handle all problems, or would freeze with no idea how to respond to a dangerous person.

You know different categories of self-defense situations are best dealt with differently. You know awareness, knowledge, and choices help keep you safe. You know how to control your body language and tone of voice and that being too passive or too aggressive creates problems. You know your voice is a self-defense tool useful both for communication and drawing attention. You know holding a weapon while creating a scene can cause an attacker to decide to leave. You know fingers-to-eyes and thigh-to-groin, done at the right time, are the most useful self-defense strikes.

You know how to read between the lines of what others say. You know how to speak strategically. You know people like others who make them feel important, but that you don't need everyone to like you. You know the importance of avoiding triggers/buttons during discussions. You know that, since people are not machines, it's impossible to fully predict how someone will react to your words or actions. You know how to dodge a question when appropriate. You know that, while you can't make someone agree with you, certain strategies can help. You know how to appear to be a good listener. In short, you know something about how deal with all people, dangerous and not, in a way that doesn't cause more problems than it solves.

Next time, in book two, you will find a chapter specifically about each of the seven people-dangers. You will learn to safely deescalate angry people. You will learn options for dealing with territorial situations. You will study how to seem a poor choice for a predator. You will learn nine helpful ways to respond to mean words. You will acquire skill in successfully striking an attacker who surprises you with a strike or grab. You'll learn to recognize and respond to predators who use deceptive strategies. You'll learn how you can help protect us all from planned mass attacks.

Later, in book three, you'll learn about defending against weapons and about protecting others. You will learn to defend from the ground, as you might need to if you fall during a self-defense situation. You will learn specific concepts and techniques related to sexual assault situations. You will learn defense against a dog and much, much more.

Now though, take some time to reflect on what you've already learned. How do you treat people differently? How do people treat you differently? Is it easier to find your voice in an emergency? Are you making safer choices? Or are you bravely able to enjoy being more adventurous? I encourage you to make a short report about what you learned from book one and share it with people who would benefit from this book or another *7 People-Dangers* book for kids, women, or men.

To find these other books, for help finding a self-defense class right for you, or to share your thoughts with me, see my website. To talk about the books on social media, use #7peopledangersbooks. For a special offer on book two, see marcyshoberg.com/bookonedone.

That's BOOK ONE DONE ! without spaces or exclamation point.

B.

Acknowledgments and Further Resources

I couldn't have written this book without help from hundreds of people who taught me, learned from me, and helped me write. I especially thank LeeAnn and Jim for help with earlier drafts.

Below are a few selected resources that relate most to this book. The next books will have a more complete list of resources I've studied, for readers interested to continue the empowering study of self-protection.

Matt Thomas is the self-defense researcher who first developed the mock-assailant class that later became Model Mugging, IMPACT, and *FAST* Defense. I appreciate the feedback and additional information he gave me about this book.

Bill Kipp, after working with Matt Thomas for a time, started *FAST* Defense. He has developed a two-hour mixed-gender armored assailant seminar which is taught at many locations in the U.S. and several elsewhere in the world.

Ellen Snortland is the author of *Beauty Bites Beast*, a book about why self-defense training is special and important for women. She is my main connection to the several IMPACT locations in the US. I will forever love IMPACT of Santa Fe, NM for opening my eyes to verbal defense and striking from sexual assault positions.

I thank Grandmaster Daniel Walker for giving me my first opportunities to teach self-defense to people of all ages; Bert and my angel for all the advice they give me; all the young and old students who've asked me thought-provoking questions during my classes and presentations; my parents for believing in me; and my kids for putting up with my shooing them away to find time to write.

Last but not least, I could never have written this book without the help and support of Tom Baca and Joseph Perea who let my students use them for practice dummies (mock assailants) and took on extra responsibility and dealt with inconveniences so I could find time to write.